D0335979

Usborne Fairytale Sticker Stor...

Little Red Riding Hood

Illustrated by Stephen Cartwright

Retold by Heather Amery and Laura Howell

How to use this book

This book tells the story of Little Red Riding Hood.
Some words in the story have been replaced by pictures.
Find the stickers that match these pictures and stick them over the top.
Each sticker has the word with it to help you read the story.

Some of the big pictures have pieces missing.
Find the stickers with the missing pieces to finish the pictures.

A yellow duck is hidden in every picture. When you have found
the duck you can put a I found the duck! sticker on the page.

Everyone liked Little Red Riding Hood.

She lived with her mother near a forest. Her

name came from the bright red

with a  that her Granny made for her.

2

"Your Granny isn't feeling well."

"Please take her this basket of   .

Go through the forest, but don't talk to

strangers," said Red Riding Hood's  .

Red Riding Hood set off.

She skipped along with her  .

Red Riding Hood didn't see a big, bad

 watching her from behind a tree.

4

Out jumped the Wolf.

"Where are you going,  ?" asked

the Wolf. "I'm taking this basket of food to my

Granny's  in the forest," she said.

"How kind you are!" said the Wolf.

He smiled a horrible smile. "Why not pick

some  for her too?"  was

a little scared. "Yes, Mr. Wolf," she said.

6

Red Riding Hood put down her basket.

She picked a big bunch of  . The

Wolf ran down the  to Granny's

cottage. He was very, very hungry.

The Wolf found Granny's cottage.

He knocked on the  . "Come in, my

dear!" called  . The Wolf ran inside

and gobbled her up in one big gulp.

I found the duck!

I found the duck!

I found the duck!

I found the duck!

Wolf

Wolf

cloak

I found the duck!

knife

I found the duck!

eyes

I found the duck!

path

food

cake

glasses

door

I found the duck!

Granny

I found the duck!

bed

Red Riding Hood

flowers

I found the duck!

woodsman

Red Riding Hood

cottage

basket

I found the duck!

hood

Wolf

I found the duck!

cottage

I found the duck!

Red Riding Hood

mother

ears

I found the duck!

flowers

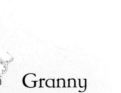

I found the duck!

I found the duck!

Granny

door

bed

Wolf

Red Riding Hood

He climbed into Granny's bed.

The Wolf put on Granny's nightcap and

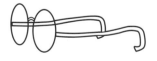 . He pulled the covers up to his

chin, and waited for  to come.

Soon, the Wolf heard Red Riding Hood.

She knocked on the  . "Come in,

my dear!" said the Wolf, in a squeaky voice.

"I'm here in my   ."

10

"Hello, Granny," said Red Riding Hood.

Then she stared. "Why, Granny, what big

 you have!" she said. "All the better

to see you with," squeaked the

Red Riding Hood felt very scared.

"But, Granny, what big   you

have!" said   . "All the better to

hear you with," squeaked the Wolf.

"And, Granny, what big teeth you have!"

"All the better to EAT you with!" said the

, and jumped out of . Red

Riding Hood screamed, but the Wolf ate her up.

13

A woodsman heard the scream.

"I'd better see if the old lady needs help," said the

 . He ran to Granny's

as fast as he could. The Wolf was asleep.

14

The woodsman killed the Wolf.

 and Red Riding Hood were inside the

Wolf. The woodsman used his  to let

them out. They were very happy to be rescued.

"Thank you for saving us!" said Granny.

"The 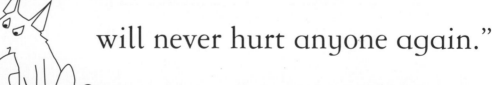 will never hurt anyone again."

And they all sat down to tea and  .

Cover design by Michael Hill   Digital manipulation by Keith Furnival and Leonard Le Rolland

First published in 2006 by Usborne Publishing Ltd, Usborne House, 83-85 Saffron Hill, London EC1N 8RT, England. www.usborne.com

Copyright © 2006 Usborne Publishing Ltd. The name Usborne and the devices 🖋 🎈 are Trade Marks of Usborne Publishing Ltd. All rights reserved.
No part of this publication may be reproduced, stored in a retrieval system, or transmitted in any form or by any means, electronic, mechanical,
photocopying, recording or otherwise without the prior permission of the publisher. First published in America in 2006. U.E. Printed in Malaysia.